Dear Parent:
Your child's love of reading starts here!

Every child learns to read in a different way and at his or her own speed. You can help your young reader improve and become more confident by encouraging his or her own interests and abilities. You can also guide your child's spiritual development by reading stories with biblical values and Bible stories, like I Can Read! books published by Zonderkidz. From books your child reads with you to the first books he or she reads alone, there are I Can Read! books for every stage of reading:

SHARED READING
Basic language, word repetition, and whimsical illustrations, ideal for sharing with your emergent reader.

BEGINNING READING
Short sentences, familiar words, and simple concepts for children eager to read on their own.

READING WITH HELP
Engaging stories, longer sentences, and language play for developing readers.

READING ALONE
Complex plots, challenging vocabulary, and high-interest topics for the independent reader.

ADVANCED READING
Short paragraphs, chapters, and exciting themes for the perfect bridge to chapter books.

I Can Read! books have introduc  ding since 1957. Featuring award-winning a fabulous cast of beloved characters, I Ca ird for beginning readers.

A lifetime of discovery begins with the magical words **"I Can Read!"**

Visit <u>www.icanread.com</u> for information on enriching your child's reading experience.
Visit <u>www.zonderkidz.com</u> for more Zonderkidz I Can Read! titles.

Always be joyful.
—*1 Thessalonians 5:16*

My Cowboy Boots
Copyright © 2002, 2008 by Crystal Bowman
Illustrations copyright © 2002 by Meredith Johnson

Requests for information should be addressed to:
Zonderkidz, *Grand Rapids, Michigan* 49530

Library of Congress Cataloging-in-Publication Data

Bowman, Crystal.
    My cowboy boots / story by Crystal Bowman ; pictures by Meredith Johnson.
       p. cm. -- (I can read! Level 1)
    Summary: A little girl wears her favorite red cowboy boots every day,
    including to church on Sunday, after asking her mother's permission.
    ISBN-13: 978-0-310-71574-0 (softcover)
    ISBN-10: 0-310-71574-1 (softcover)
    [1. Boots--Fiction. 2. Christian life--Fiction. 3. Mother and child--Fiction. 4.
    Stories in rhyme.] I. Johnson, Meredith, ill. II. Title.
PZ8.3.B6773Myc 2008
[E]--dc22

                      2007023107

All Scripture quotations, unless otherwise indicated, are taken from the HOLY BIBLE, NEW INTERNATIONAL READER'S VERSION ®. Copyright © 1995, 1996, 1998 by International Bible Society. Used by permission of Zondervan. All Rights Reserved.

Art Direction: Jody Langley
Cover Design: Sarah Molegraaf

Printed in China

08 09 10 • 4 3 2 1

My Cowboy Boots

story by Crystal Bowman
pictures by Meredith Johnson

See my new red cowboy boots?

I wear them every day.

I wear them when I eat.

I wear them when I play.

My feet are very happy.

They like it that way.

I wear my boots on Monday.

We go to Mama's store.

Click, clack, go my boots

as I skip right through the door.

Click, clack,

Click, clack,

8

across the tile floor.

I wear my boots on Tuesday

out to the tire swing.

My dog and cat come with me.

And God can hear me sing.

I swing way up.

I swing way down.

I feel like I can fly.

I wear my boots on Wednesday

to ride the rodeo.

I hop on my big pony.

Giddy-up! Here we go!

I giddy-up fast.

I giddy-up slow.

Whoa, pony, whoa!

I wear my boots on Thursday

to eat my yummy snack.

Mama put peanut butter

and crackers in a sack.

I like to lick my fingers.

I give my lips a smack!

I wear my boots on Friday

to sing a happy song.

"Jesus loves me. This I know."

My red boots march along.

My boots are on my feet.

That's where they belong.

I wear my boots on Saturday
to bounce my great big ball.

I bounce it on the floor.

I bounce it off the wall.

My ball goes way, way up.

And then I let it fall.

I wear my boots on Sunday

to go to church and pray.

I asked my mama if I could.

She said it was okay.

My feet are very happy.

They like it that way.